My thanks to:
Marie Gravage, without whose critical ear this
book could not have been completed.

Pete Parente, without whose energy and encouragement,
the manuscript would have remained on the shelf.

Pat Brice, Lynn Hartsell, Betty Platco, Maida Parr
Bobbi Wright, Kristi Youngdahl, Zu Vincent, Sheila Jansen,
Mona Locke, Joy Helsing, Audrey Small and all the other
poets and writers who have been involved in my work.

Tree Of Life Publishing
P.O. BOX 421004
Summerland Key, Fl 33042

Published by Tree Of Life Publishing 2004.

Printed in Hong Kong.

Library of Congress Control Number: 2004104400

Doro, Ann
The Missing Canary/ by Ann Doro: jacket by Tim Young

ISBN 0-9745052-2-6

THE MISSING CANARY
A Toot Sweet Mystery

Story by
Ann Doro

Jacket illustrated and designed by
Tim Young

Tree Of Life Publishing

1

When Sandy Carpenter rode her bike into the driveway on Friday afternoon, her mother's car was already there.

"Practice took longer tonight," she called as she ran up the steps, yanking off the baseball cap she always wore to protect her freckled face from the sun. "I think I've made it. Pitching, I mean. First string." She was almost inside the door when she heard Mrs. Barnes, the next door neighbor, screaming.

"Billy," she cried out. "He's not at home. He should have been here two hours ago. You ride the same bus," she said to Sandy. "Did you see him get off anywhere?"

"I don't ride the bus on Friday," Sandy said. The whole neighborhood knew Sandy was determined to pitch for the Gainsburg Junior Gophers. The name, the coach had explained, meant this team really dug in. The town sponsored both the Junior and Senior Gophers. Any kid who played during the spring school season, and who kept his or her grades up, could play all summer on the town teams.

Mrs. Barnes came into the yard. "I've already called the bus people. They're sure he *did* get on. But the driver says he doesn't remember seeing him get off anywhere." The woman clasped her hands together in a nervous gesture, then brushed her hair back and put both hands on the sides of her head. "I suppose, with all those kids on the bus, the driver wouldn't pay much attention to *one* little boy. She started up the steps then stopped to glance down the block. "I don't know what to do."

Mrs. Carpenter appeared at the door. "Come in, Emma," she said. "We'll call the police."

"I'll go look for Billy," Sandy said. He was her "little buddy" in Mrs. Dunn's afternoon kindergarten class. On Fridays, eighth graders spent an hour in that classroom, working with the little kids. She liked Billy, and didn't want him to be in any kind of trouble. As she wheeled her bike out the gate, she called back, "I'll get Tim to help."

Tim was her closest friend, though her girl friends didn't understand why. Tim was considered a "nerd" because he spent more time at his computer than other kids did in front of the TV. Sandy, on the other hand, would rather play baseball than eat. But she and Tim had one thing in common. They wanted to be detectives, and read every mystery they could put their hands on.

"Hey," she yelled as she approached his house. It was their password. Whenever they had something important to share, they yelled, "Hey".

As she knew he would, Tim popped out his door and raced down the steps. "Yeah?" he asked.

"We've got something to investigate," she told him, and added, "Billy Barnes didn't come home on the bus today. His mother's almost over the edge."

"Right," Tim said, yelling back, "I have to go somewhere, Mom." He grabbed his bike. Sandy could hear his mother say, "Don't be too long," and Tim answered, "OK." When he joined Sandy, he asked, "Any idea where to start looking?"

Sandy was thoughtful. "He asked for the word 'secret' today, wanted me to write it on his picture. Maybe that secret has something to do with where he went instead of coming home."

"What was the picture?" Tim asked.

"A horse. In front of a big barn."

They both said it at the same time. "Mr. Melvin's farm." They had ridden his horses several times. He had three, and rented them by the hour to any kid whose allowance would pay for it. Billy had always wanted to ride one, too, and talked to Sandy endlessly about the time his class visited the farm. It was at the edge of town.

"Shouldn't take long," Sandy said.

They rode off as fast as they could, turning right at the end of Second Street, past the market, the newspaper office, the bank. On they hurried, past the video rental place, the TV repair shop and the drug store. When they turned on Hill Street, Sandy said, "The bus stops here. It's probably where Billy got off."

"It's still about a mile out there," Tim said. "Think a kid as little as Billy could walk that far?"

"He's totally into horses," Sandy said. "Wanting to see them would keep him walking. It won't take us long to find out."

When they arrived, there was not a single horse in the yard near the barn. Inside, they looked down the row of open stalls where the cattle were lined up at milking time. No Billy. The cows chewed on the grain they had been fed. One turned to look at them, then lowered its head to take another chomp. Toward the back of the barn were the three horse stalls. They saw no horses. Checking each stall, Sandy looked at Tim, shaking her head.

"You don't suppose he's sold them, do you?" she asked.

"They sure aren't here," Tim said, "but get a load of this."

Curled up on a bale of hay at the back of the third stall was the missing boy.

"Billy, wake up," Sandy said.

The boy opened his eyes and blinked. "Thunder's gone," he said. Thunder was the big black one, the one in Billy's picture, Sandy remembered.

"And so are you. Not home, at least. Come on," Tim said.

"Your mom's worried sick about you." Sandy reached out to take Billy's hand. The little boy looked at them blankly, still half-asleep. "He's gone," he said again. "I wanted to feed him this." He pulled a piece of carrot from his pocket. Tears came to his eyes. "But he's not here."

Grasping his hand, Sandy said, "Come on, Billy. We have to get you home before your mother goes into orbit."

Tim said, "Yeah, buddy. We can talk about horses some other time."

They had started back, Billy riding on the seat of Tim's bicycle while Tim stood on the pedals, when a police car approached.

Stopping, the officer leaned out his window. "What are you kids up to?" he asked.

"This is Billy Barnes," Sandy said, and explained to the officer about Billy's "secret".

"Quick thinking," the man said, smiling at the two

investigators who had solved the case. "I'd better give him a ride home. His mother's frantic about the kid."

"But I want to stay with them," Billy said. "I like to ride on a big kid's bike."

"Got to get you home faster than that," the officer said. " I'll let you blow the siren. Just once, though. Can't have folks thinking we're having a crime wave in Gainsburg."

Billy ran to get into the patrol car. Sandy grinned at Tim when she heard the siren scream. "Just once, like the man said," she commented. She and Tim headed home. At her gate, she asked, "Want to eat with us? Mom's making pizza, and she's way better than Antonio's Pizza Palace."

"I'll ask my mom," Tim said as he hurried toward home. Eating was another big favorite with the two would be detectives.

2

The next day, a reporter from the Gainsburg Bulletin knocked at Sandy's door. "I'm here to interview the two kids who rescued Billy Barnes," he said.

"Rescued?" Sandy said. "All we did was think where he'd most likely go."

"Cop said something about how you knew Billy's secret."

"Let me call Tim," Sandy said. "He's in on this, too." Instead of reaching for the telephone, she startled the reporter by going out the front door and yelling an ear-bursting "Hey." The reporter showed further surprised when, less than five minutes later Tim appeared at the door.

"Let's sit out on the porch," suggested Sandy. "It's such a nice day. And we can show you Billy's house, in case you want to take pictures."

"Photographer will be by later," the reporter said. "I think he'd like a shot of you two with little Billy."

"Don't call him 'little Billy' in the story," Sandy said. "He's almost six, and wants us to think of him as 'big'."

"Right," said the reporter.

"You could say Billy walked a whole mile," Tim said. "He'd keep the clipping to show his grandkids."

When the reporter had taken notes on all the details, he said, "Look for the story on the front page of tomorrow's paper."

Later, the camera man did arrive, taking so many shots Tim asked, "How many do you need for the article?"

"One," the man said. "But it's got to be just right. One more. Billy, you look up at Sandy and Tim, like they're your best friends."

"Sandy's my big buddy," Billy said, smiling up at her.

"Great," said the photographer. "That'll do it."

Dad was proud of his daughter when he showed her the Sunday edition, with a headline reading "Students Solve Mystery of Missing Boy". "Looks like you may get involved in detective work, after all. Though I hope you'll put it on hold. I'm looking forward to reading your name on the sports page."

Sandy ran to ask Tim if he'd seen the paper. He had. And was involved in reading another headlined story. "Mr. Melvin Reports Stolen Horse."

"Look here," he said, pointing to the second paragraph, which read, *Mr. Melvin says he sold two horses last week to a Middleton man. The third he had planned to keep, since children enjoyed riding Thunder, a black horse who was more gentle than his name would suggest.*

"That explains why we didn't see any horses Friday," she

said. "Maybe we should try to locate Thunder for Mr. Melvin."

Sandy knew she had to get home. Her family liked to drive out into the country on Sunday. At Tim's gate, she paused, waving for him to look down the street. In front of her house stood a black and white car. The chief of police was getting out. Together, they walked slowly toward it.

"So you're the two who used such quick thinking Friday, locating the missing boy," the man said.

"We didn't do anything special," Tim began.

Sandy nodded agreement. "He's our neighbor," she said. "We know him pretty well, and all we did was… ."

"Figure out where he'd be likely to go," Tim finished.

"That kind of thinking makes a successful policeman," the chief said. "You may have a future in our department. I just want to add my thanks for a job well done."

After he had gone, Tim and Sandy looked at each other.

"Future?" Tim said. "Why does it have to be 'future'?"

"Right," Sandy agreed.   "We're good at solving things. Reading all those mysteries must have taught us something."

"We could advertise," Tim said. "I can make up business cards on my computer."

"Have our own business?"

"Why not?" Tim asked.

"We'd need a name," Sandy said. "Something rad."

"How about the ASAP Detective Agency?"

"Why ASAP?" Sandy wanted to know.

"It means… ."

"I know what it means. Toot Sweet."

"Huh?"

"It's French, meaning right away or sooner. I can't spell the French, but we should do it in American anyway. So clients will know what it means."

"Toot Sweet," Tim said, as if tasting the words. "It is a grabber"

"You can be Tim Toot. I'll be Sandy Sweet." Sandy grinned. "Picture it. MYSTERY'S OUR BEAT. NEED SOMETHING FOUND? CALL TOOT SWEET."

"We'd better get on it," Tim said. "Do you have to go with your folks today?"

"Maybe not," Sandy said. "I'll tell them we've got work to do."

That was how the TOOT SWEET DETECTIVE AGENCY began.

3

"We can use my old playhouse for an office," Sandy said. "I hardly ever use it any more. Haven't played in it since I was ten."

"So now that you're old as that guy in the bible... ."

"I'll be fourteen next month." Sandy glared at Tim.

"Still just a kid. I was fourteen last November."

"We going to stand here arguing about ages, or get to work?" Sandy scowled. Then like mist in the morning, her irritation vanished. She was eager to get started.

"What's first, oh great leader?" Tim asked with a grin.

"Business cards. That's your department. You're good at art, so make one with a picture, one about detectives. I'll get all the kid stuff out of the office."

Tim left, and Sandy walked back to the playhouse,

excited at this new way to use a house she *really did* love. It had been fun playing here, with her girlfriends, when she was a kid. But now she and Tim had more important stuff to do.

Sorting things out, she packed the toy dish set in a box, together with the dolls that had slept on the little bed for six or seven years. Toy cooking pans, a mixer, a cookie cutter, all stored in the oven that really baked, could stay where they were for now. Why bother to find a box for them?

"Too bad the furniture isn't bigger," she said. "These chairs are Billy's size." Sighing, she told herself, "We'll have a sale. Should earn enough to buy some office furniture."

There *was* the crate she'd used as storage for make-believe groceries. It would do for bookshelves, if they needed any. When everything was packed, she started carrying things out to the garage. Once that was done, she began making "Yard Sale" signs, then remembered Tim could do it better on his computer.

When Tim came back, she showed him the boxes and said, "We'll have a sale next Saturday. And buy a desk for our office. Other stuff, too, maybe."

"How about a phone line?" he asked. "So I can put my computer in, and use the internet?"

"Cost too much, at least right away," Sandy guessed. "And don't you need your computer at home?"

"We gotta be in the office if we're going to tend to business," Tim said. "We can do our homework while we're waiting for clients. But here," he said, holding out a card. "Think this'll do?"

The card had a magnifying glass pictured with an eye behind it. The card read, TOOT SWEET DETECTIVE AGENCY. No Case Too Big Or Small. Call Sandy Sweet at 837-4944, or Tim Toot at 837-9881.

"Perfect." Sandy was more excited than ever. "Let's make flyers, too, the same as these, only bigger. I've got some colored paper to print them on. We need a desk big enough for your computer, and a place to put our cards." She rummaged through a box and found a big scallop shell she'd picked up at the beach last summer when her family had gone to Marina Del Sol. "This can hold the cards," she said.

"Need a place for a phone, when our business can pay for it," Tim added.

"Can you make some yard sale signs?" Sandy asked. "If we sell all this stuff, we'll have money for things we need."

"Right," Tim agreed. He was off again. When he came back he had flyers and sale signs. He was dragging an old student desk. "Not very big," he said. "But it'll do until we can buy a better one."

On Monday after school, they began distributing flyers. As they rode past Billy's house, they heard him crying. Standing on the porch, he was staring inside the open window at the stand that had held a bird cage.

"What's wrong?" Sandy asked.

"My c-c-c-canary," he said, crying louder.

"Did it die?"

"No. It's g-g-g-gone."

"Gone?" Tim asked. "Where?"

"I don't know."

"Did it get out of its cage?"

"No." Billy tried to stop crying so he could talk. "That's gone, too."

"The cage?" Sandy asked in a puzzled voice. "Did your parents do something with it?"

"No." Billy began crying again.

"Where was it when you last saw it?" Tim asked.

"There." Billy pointed up at the hook on the stand where the cage had been hung.

"When was that? Today?" Sandy asked.

Billy sniffed and nodded. "It was there when I went to school."

"Weird," said Tim.

"Our first case," Sandy said. She was handing a flyer to Billy when Mrs. Barnes came out. She gave it to Billy's mother instead.

"I called the police," she said. "But you two are good at finding missing things, including--" She patted her son on the shoulder-- "missing boys. Do you think you can find his bird? He loves it so. I guess we shouldn't have left it by an open window. But who would steal a canary?"

"It's a tough question," Sandy said thoughtfully. "It doesn't make any sense."

"I don't suppose it could be just a mean trick some kid is playing," Tim wondered out loud.

"Billy doesn't have any kids who don't like him." That was Sandy's polite way of telling Tim it was a ridiculous idea.

"Can you find Twinby?" Billy asked. He began to look more hopeful, as if the two who had found him when Thunder was gone could do anything.

"We'll certainly try," Sandy assured him.

"We'll begin our investigation right away," Tim said

Parking their bikes, Sandy and Tim walked around the neighborhood to ask people if they knew anything about the missing bird. No one had anything helpful to tell them until they talked to the little girl in the yard next to Billy's. She was chasing her puppy around the big old oak tree. In the back yard, Sandy noticed the swing was still moving back and forth. Mona must have just jumped out of it. They went to interview her as a possible witness.

"We're looking for Billy's canary," Sandy told her. "Did you see anyone near it?"

"Someone who took the cage, too," Tim added.

Mona shook her head. Then she screwed up her face, as if trying to remember something. She said, "There was that funny man."

"Funny? How?"

"He walked on his tiptoes."

"Like kids do when they don't want their parents to know what they're doing?" Tim asked.

"Sort of."

"Where was he?"

"He went up Billy's steps, and on the porch. Tip toe, tip toe." Mona laughed.

"What did he do then?" Sandy asked.

"I don't know."

"You didn't watch him?"

"Mommie called me to eat lunch."

"So we know about when he was here," Tim said thoughtfully. "Was he big?"

"Uh huh. Big up, not around."

Sandy mused, "We can look for a tall thin man."

"Was he old?" Tim asked.

"Sort of."

"Mona," called Mrs. Kent from the porch. "Come get in the car. I have to get some things at the store."

Mona hurried toward the driveway, leaving Sandy and Tim to review what they had learned.

"Old, to Mona, could be a kid in sixth grade," Sandy said. "But we do know he's probably tall and thin."

"What kind of creep would steal a little kid's bird?" Tim wanted to know.

"How'd they get away with it in broad daylight? Think about it. They took cage and all. Why?"

"Maybe we're up against a gang of professional criminals," Tim said.

Sandy almost said, *Don't be silly.* Then she wondered if he might be right. Surely no petty thief would bother with a canary . But what would a criminal even want with a canary?

"What was it that cop said?" she asked. "Something about not wanting people to think there's a crime wave in town?"

"A missing horse. Now a missing canary. Something's up," Tim thought out loud.

They walked out onto the sidewalk and, as they were passing Billy's house, he called, "Did you find Twinby yet?"

"Not yet," Tim said.

"But we have our first clue," Sandy said.

"Billy," said his mother, coming out to take him by the hand. "We have to let the detectives do their work. We did call the police too, you know."

Tim and Sandy looked at each other. Both winked at the same time, as if to say *When Billy was missing, she called the police. But who found him?*

"Grown ups forget how much kids can do. But we'll show them," Tim said as they walked away.

They went on to deliver flyers to the library, the bulletin board outside the market, the one at the drug store, and asked at the video rental shop if they could leave their ads on the counter.

"Where else?" asked Tim.

"Maybe we can post one on the bulletin board outside the principal's office," Sandy said. "He always encourages kids to find jobs to earn extra spending money."

"Think the kids'll just consider it a joke?"

"What, our being in business? Well, if they do, they'll soon learn to take us seriously when we solve the case of the missing canary."

Sandy spoke as if she had no doubt they'd have the canary back before evening. It did not prove to be that easy.

4

"We've got a missing bird," Tim said, "and we have a pretty good idea who took it."

"We do?" Sandy asked, raising her eyebrows.

"Yeah. A tall thin man. In Gainsburg, where tall and thin doesn't happen every day, he should stand out like a stubbed toe."

"And you think whoever stole the canary is hanging around, waiting for us to walk up, tap him on the arm and say, 'The bird you took belongs to a nice little kid. So give it back.' Right?"

"That's not what I said. I'm just reviewing the evidence."

"Maybe we should start by checking with pet stores," Sandy told him.

"I doubt if anybody's dumb enough to steal a canary just to try to sell it again," Tim said. "What store'd buy it?"

"That's not what I mean. Somebody wanted one enough to steal it in daylight, when anyone might have seen him. Risky, don't you think. If someone caught him coming down the steps with the cage in his hand, seems to me it would be embarrassing trying to explain what he was up to."

"Oh, he could say, 'I was walking by and saw this great looking bird. I don't know what came over me. I just wanted to get a better look at it.'"

"And Santa flies an ox cart." Sandy's expression let Tim know she wasn't about to take him seriously.

"Well, what... ?" Tim began.

"I just mean-- if someone needed a canary that much, maybe he tried to buy one first."

"Oh." Tim scratched his elbow, which was his way of concentrating. "I guess you have a point. I'll get my bike." Then he thought for a moment. "It's a long ride to Exeter, and that's the only place around that has a pet store."

Sandy smiled. "You know what the phone company says. 'Let your fingers do the walking.' We can look in the phone book."

Checking, they found two pet stores listed. The first one they called specialized in tropical fish, and had puppies for sale. They didn't have much call for birds, they said. The other store did carry birds, but claimed no one wanted to buy canaries. Kids, they had found, would rather have parakeets or mynah birds.

"Well," Tim said as they went out onto the porch, "nobody would be dumb enough to steal a canary to give to his kid, when he could buy a parakeet for a few bucks."

"Right. Somebody needed Billy's canary. But why?" Sandy was perplexed. "They used to take canaries down into mines," she reflected. "To make sure there was enough oxygen for the miners to breathe. I read that when we had to do reports in fourth grade. When there wasn't enough oxygen, canaries would drop dead. But who...?"

"Don't suppose they're opening that old gold mine up in the hills again?" Tim asked. "I haven't heard about it, if they are. Be fun, though. They used to say it was haunted, didn't they?"

"Maybe it's about to become haunted again," Sandy said. "By ghosts who have to have oxygen to breathe." She sat on the edge of the porch and swung her legs back and forth. "Seems to me, if the mine is going to be opened again, they'd have modern methods of measuring the oxygen down there."

"Besides," Tim asked, "who'd steal a kid's bird if they're on the level."

"Maybe that little girl's back from the store. She might remember something else that will help."

Mona was sitting on the porch swing, holding her dog. When Sandy and Tim came up the steps, she said, "This is Pokey. Like in the book." She held up her right hand, fingers spread wide. "I'm five years old. I get to go to school pretty soon, like Billy."

"You're a big girl," Sandy agreed. "Are you big enough to remember what the man was wearing. You know, the funny one on Billy's porch?"

The little girl screwed up her face again, thinking. "Pants like George's," she said. "Except George wears blue."

"Jeans, you mean?" asked Tim.

"Mm hmm."

"And this man...?" Tim started to ask.

"Black. Dirty. But black."

"Not like the pants your daddy wears to work?" Sandy asked.

"No. Jeans like George wears. Only black." The puppy jumped down and ran off the porch. "George's are clean, unless he has to dig up plants." Mona seemed to feel important, being asked questions about a mystery by these *big* kids.

George, Sandy knew, took care of everybody's lawn in the neighborhood, except for Mrs. Jeremy, who liked to plant bulbs, and didn't have grass to mow.

"Did you notice how the man got here? Did he walk up the street?"

The little girl frowned. "There was truck, I think. Right in front of Billy's house."

"You're a good witness," Sandy told Mona. "You remember a lot of things. What color was the truck?"

"White-- I think."

"A pickup? Like George's?"

"Kinda. But different."

"Different? How?"

"Like Jenny's. You could sleep in it."

"A camper shell, I'd guess," Tim said to Sandy.

"Thank you, Mona. You've helped us a lot. If you think of any other things, will you have your mom call us?" Sandy handed the little girl one of their business cards. Mona studied it as if she could read.

"Funny picture," she said, putting the card in the pocket of her shorts.

"I hope that card doesn't go through the laundry," Sandy said as she and Tim walked toward home. When they passed Billy's house, he called out, "Did you find Twinby yet?"

"Not yet," Sandy said.

"We're working on it, "Tim added.

When Tim headed toward his house he asked, "Wanta

eat with us? Mom's frying chicken the way you like."

"With that yummy gravy?"

"What else? Ask your mom."

Sandy dashed home, and was back in minutes. "This'll give us more time to consider our clues," she said.

"Not at the table," Tim warned. "We gotta keep what they call it--client's confidential, or something like that. Besides, Dad always tells what happened at the office. We can talk in my room after."

Another day drew to a close in the life of Gainsburg's latest private eyes.

5

Tuesday afternoon, Sandy went to Tim's after practice. They would be staying after on Tuesdays and Fridays, Coach had said, for an hour and a half. Until school was out. Then they'd have daily practice, except for Saturdays, when the Gophers had games scheduled. Sunday was still family day. No games, no practice.

"You've got a good arm," the coach had said. "Almost as good as Biff Larson's. Too bad he got into such a jam."

Sandy remembered Biff, sort of. She'd been in sixth grade when he tried to steal stuff from the high school. That was what people had said, anyway.

"Any ideas?" Tim asked when he answered her knock. No "Hey" today. Nothing was that important, except for getting on with the investigation.

"Tomorrow we can ride the bus to school, and walk home," Sandy said.

"Walk?" Tim growled. "Why walk? Bikes are faster."

"But we can look for a white pickup with a camper shell. We'll see more if we're walking."

"All right," he agreed, but he didn't seem too happy about it. Then he brightened. "We can finish putting our flyers around."

"Yard sale signs, too," Sandy said. "I can't wait to get a regular desk."

On Wednesday afternoon, they met in front of the school and started walking.

"Let's do Grover's Market first," Sandy suggested. "Maybe Mr. Grover will remember whether anyone asked about a canary lately. He sells bird seed, you know."

"Nope," the grocer said when they asked. "Nobody said anything about a canary. Mrs. Barnes bought food for Billy's bird couple days ago, is all."

Asked if he'd seen a tall thin man wearing dirty black jeans, he shook his head. "Not that I can... Wait. There were a couple of guys in here buying beer. I pretty much know all my customers-- but these guys... Come to think of it, that thin guy looked a lot like... ." He shook his head again, then scratched his head and said, "If I didn't know Biff Larson was in juvenile hall, I'd say it might be him."

"Biff Larson?" Sandy felt a rush of excitement. "Funny. The coach mentioned him just yesterday."

"Two guys?" Tim asked.

"I think there were three."

"Didn't happen to see what they were driving, did you?" asked Tim.

"No. Why all the questions?"

"Billy's canary's been stolen. We're trying to find it for him." Sandy turned to go, then stopped. "Were those guys here when Mrs. Barnes bought the bird seed?"

"Maybe so. Hard to remember, when it doesn't seem important."

"It may be *very* important," Tim said. To Sandy, he said, "Could be Biff Larson is back. *He'd* steal a kid's canary. And he'd know where the Barnes house is."

As they walked away, Sandy could hardly contain her enthusiasm. "Three guys. One of them *could* be Biff."

"He'd be mean enough to steal from a kid." Tim doubled up his fists and said, "He used to knock off my glasses. On purpose. I'd like to punch him right in the nose."

When they passed the TV repair shop, they saw a white pickup. *With a camper shell.* On its side was a sign, Gainsburg TV and Repair.

"Mona didn't say anything about a sign on the side," Sandy said.

"Don't they have magnetic signs you can stick on, or take off?" Tim wondered out loud.

They nodded to each other and headed toward the store. Mr. Elwin came out just as they got to the door. He worked for Mr. Larson.

"Sorry, kids. Gotta go out on a call," the man said.

"Is Mr. Larson here?" Sandy asked.

"No. He's out of town right now."

"Does anyone besides you drive this truck?" Tim asked.

"Hey, kids, I gotta get going. Why all the questions, anyway?"

"We're looking for Biff," Sandy said.

"That kid. He's nothing but trouble." The man got in.

"Haven't seen him." He drove away.

Sandy said, "I'll bet we can find out more when Mr. Larson gets back. Biff Larson. I still remember the day he sneaked into our school and turned on the fire alarm. I guess he thought it was a blast to see all the kids and teachers lined up on the playground."

"He didn't just turn on a fire alarm. I think... ."

"Wasn't that the time the high school principal got a call about a bomb in the computer lab?" Sandy asked.

"And why Biff got sent to juvie, I think," Tim said.

"Right. He was trying to steal sports equipment out of the gym while everybody was outside and the cops were looking for the bomb."

"Funny part was," Tim said, chuckling, "he walked right into them as he was trying to get away."

"He doesn't seem to be overloaded with brains," Sandy said. "Guess he could be back home now. I heard, though, that he had been out. Got mixed up with some other guys--a hold up at one of those service station markets? Got sent back, didn't he?"

Tim kicked at a pebble. "Yeah, I think so." He frowned as he asked, " If he is back now, what would some kid just out of juvie need with a canary."

"We don't know *for sure* he's the one," Sandy said.

"Right. We don't know *for sure* the white pickup is the TV repair truck."

"Tomorrow, let's go by there again," Sandy suggested. "If nobody's in it, maybe we can find out if the sign on the side comes off."

"And whether Biff gets to take it for a spin now and then."

"Would he be likely to take a horse for a spin, too?"

Tim stopped, looked at Sandy and said, "Thunder, you

think?"

"Again, why? What would he need with a--canary and a horse?" Suddenly Sandy grabbed Tim's arm. "The mine. It's up in the hills, and nobody ever bothered to put a road in to it."

Tim looked at her blankly.

"It's a *gold* mine," she explained.

"I know that! You don't think... ."

"I don't know. But isn't it weird to have a horse and a canary missing at the same time. A horse would come in handy to carry equipment to the mine."

"We can check it out," Tim said. "Take a bus up to Ghost Town Flats, maybe."

"First, I think we should follow the lead on Biff Larson. If he's the thief, there must be somebody in it with him."

Tim scratched his head. "Think he'd try to work the mine? Heavy duty, if you ask me."

"Who knows *what* a guy like Biff is willing to do?" Sandy started walking. "Let's see what we can find out tomorrow."

The two detectives walked home in silence.

6

Thursday Tim and Sandy rode their bikes to school. "I can't see walking again," he reasoned. "We want to look at the pickup, and we *know* where it is."

"Okay," Sandy agreed. "I'd rather be riding, too."

On the way to the TV repair shop after school, they passed the bank. A tall thin stranger came out. He looked up and down the street several times, as if studying it. For what purpose, Sandy wondered as she pulled to the curb and went, "Hey", in a soft voice.

"No black jeans," Tim observed.

"Scruffy looking though. Sort of."

"Yeah, but Sandy. Look at the guy's boots. He'd clomp, even on tiptoes."

"I guess," Sandy agreed. "Still, he's a stranger. Could have worn sneakers."

The man walked past them and stopped to look in the hardware store window.

"We can ask about him at the bank," Sandy said.

Inside the bank, all the tellers were busy. Mr. Graves, just coming out of his office, was saying to his secretary, "I'm leaving a little early today. Can you get in at seven tomorrow?"

"Sure. What's happening?"

"Remember that bank robbery about five years ago down in Layton County? Seems some of the money from that robbery is beginning to surface in nearby towns."

Tim and Sandy shot each other a knowing glance. They hurried out and down the street. Stopping, they peered into the hardware store.

"Don't see him," Tim said.

"Let's go in and ask Mr. Healy about the guy."

The hardware man was counting cash from the register. Tim and Sandy went to the counter. "That man, " Sandy began.

Pausing to look at them, Mr. Healy said, "What man?"

"The tall, thin man. The one that was just in here," Tim said.

"Just looking around," Mr. Healy said.

"Have you ever seen him before? Did he say anything to you?"

"Why the curiosity about a stranger?" Mr. Healy looked at them intently. "Aren't you the kids who found that little boy? I saw your picture in the paper." He grinned. "What? You on another case?"

"Yep," Tim said. "We're looking into the disappearance of Mr. Melvin's horse and Billy Barnes' canary."

"So, did he say anything to you?" Sandy could hardly

contain her impatience.

"Well--he said he was building a fence. Asked about nails that wouldn't rust."

Sandy shot a glance at Tim. They both said at the same time, "Corral." Sandy added, "Maybe he's got to build some place to keep the horse."

Mr. Healy smiled. "Kids, nobody can hide a horse in a corral. I just didn't get the feeling he was the criminal type. I think you'd better refocus your investigation."

Standing in front of the hardware store, Sandy said, "I think he fits into the picture. I don't know how. I just feel it."

Tim agreed. "Why don't we head back to the repair shop and see if Mr. Elwin is there." But the store was locked. The truck was gone. Disappointed, they headed home.

"Maybe our folks can tell us if Biff's out of juvie," Sandy said. "It does seem like he's our best lead."

"We gotta remember, he's innocent until proven guilty. That's the law." Tim looked serious as he added, "He may have cleaned up his act. Maybe he's going to help in his dad's business."

"Right," Sandy agreed.

That evening, her father told Sandy Biff *had* come home, that his father was hoping he was ready to settle down.

"Larson did the best he could with Biff. Pretty hard to raise a kid by yourself. The mother died when Biff was four."

Maybe he was mad at other kids for having a mother, Sandy thought. *Maybe that was why he was so mean to kids littler than he was.* She considered how life would be if her own mother were gone. The idea was a heavy one. She wanted to talk it out with Tim.

Knocking on his door, she said a quiet, "Hey," when he opened it.

"Got something?" he asked, his eyes lighting up.

"Sort of. Not a clue, though." She told her partner what she had learned about Biff. "As kids, we wouldn't think about that," she said. "But it does help *explain* why he was such a stink pot."

"He wouldn't get much mothering in juvie," Tim observed. "Still, it *could* change his attitude. Wouldn't be much fun in there. Might be worth shaping up."

"Or he could still be hooked up with those other guys, you know. It does seem iffy that a horse and a canary are missing *right now*."

"We'll have to keep trying at the TV shop, I guess. It's our best lead."

"Don't forget, we have a sale to do. Saturday. Early." Sandy *was* the practical one.

"How early is early?" Tim wanted to know.

"Oh, sixish."

Tim groaned.

7

Saturday morning, Sandy displayed her old toys on boxes
and on the card table from the den. Tim added his used puzzles,
two computer games, a tricycle he had ridden when he was four,
and a toy dog that looked like the puppy Mona had been holding.
Sandy's mother added an old TV and a book on tape that taught
Spanish. At seven, they were ready. At eight, they ate the break-
fast Sandy's mother brought to them on trays. At nine, Tim glared
at Sandy.

"Your bright idea, wasn't it?"

Sandy was about to tell him what she thought of his
attitude, when she was interrupted by the arrival of their first
customers, Mona and her mother.

"Mona loves dolls," Mrs. Kent said. "And toy dogs." The
little girl had already

gathered a Raggedy Ann doll and Tim's stuffed dog.

"Can I have these dishes, too?" Mona begged.

"I guess so," her mother agreed, handing Sandy a ten dollar bill. As cashier, the girl counted out some coins and bills, but Mrs. Keys said, "Keep the change. I understand it's for a good cause."

"We're starting our own business," Tim said. "Sandy and I are detectives."

"Yes. You found Billy when he wandered off. And now, I understand you're trying to find his canary."

"That's right," Sandy said. "Mona gave us our first clue."

The little girl stood as tall as she could. "I'm a big girl now," she said.

"Thank you," Sandy said as mother and daughter left, a smile stretching wide across Mona's happy face. Others arrived, and for several hours, she and Tim were too busy to talk about anything but their sale. They heard comments from some of their customers.

"These are the kids who…," or "Kids should be rewarded for…," or "The newspaper should have carried a story about this sale."

"I guess our business is on its way," Tim said when the rush of buyers eased off.

Sandy smiled as she counted the money they had taken in. "Our treasury now has forty-seven dollars and eighty cents," she said. "I saw a desk in the window of the THRIFTY SHOPPER for forty. Maybe we can get it."

There were only a few items left to deal with. These they stored in the Carpenter garage.

"Might have another sale in a month or two," Sandy said. "By that time, we may find other stuff we need to get rid of." She liked selling things almost as much as Tim liked working at his computer. Tim grunted, and he didn't smile.

"So how about the desk," she asked, after they had put everything away.

"That forty-seven dollars and eighty cents burning a hole in your pocket?" Tim asked, grinning.

"Huh?"

"That's what my grandpa used to say. If you earn it, right away you gotta spend it."

Sandy glared at Tim. "We *need* a desk."

"I was only kidding. But how'll we get it here? Those guys don't deliver, or if they do, it'll be too expensive."

"Uncle Jim has a truck," Sandy said. "I'll bet he'd pick it up for us."

She phoned, and her uncle agreed to meet them at the thrift store. They arrived just as the manager was about to lock up.

"Please," Sandy begged. "We need that desk for our business."

The woman looked at Sandy's uncle, who grinned but added, "These two are in business. They're private eyes."

"I see," the woman said. As if she understood how much they needed the desk, she opened the door again. "For a new business," she said, "we have a slight discount." She charged them thirty-five dollars. "Mrs. Barnes works here Wednesdays, as a volunteer," she said, "She told me how you located her son."

When the desk was loaded on the truck, Sandy and Tim climbed up beside Uncle Jim and they headed for home. Fortunately, her father was there to help unload it.

"Where do you want this thing?" he asked. "In the playhouse?"

"Not the *playhouse*, Daddy. The *office*."

"We need to make a sign for the door," Tim said as they approached the building, but no one seemed to hear him.

Sandy pointed to a spot in the middle of the room. "There," she said. "I think that's the best place for it."

"Nope," Tim argued. "Gotta have it near the phone line."

"We don't have a phone line," Sandy reminded him.

"But we will," he insisted.

"When we do, we can make this our phone stand," she said, dragging the student desk into a corner.

Tim glanced around, then pointed to an electric outlet on the wall of the area that had been the "kitchen". "There," he said. "I can plug in my computer, at least."

When the desk was in place, Sandy gave her uncle and her father big hugs. "Thanks," she said. "Thanks a bunch."

Tim shook hands with both men and added his thanks. When the two partners were alone in their office, Tim said, "I'm going to get some paint and put a sign on the door. What should it say?"

"Toot Sweet Detective Agency. What else?"

"I mean, do we need a word like 'office'?"

"I don't see why," Sandy said. She went to the door. "While you're doing that, I'm going to collect the sale signs. We can save them for next time."

"Yeah. Next time, we can sell all our mystery stories," Tim agreed. "We don't need to read about them any more. We'll be able to write our own."

As she started off, Tim said, "Wait. I want to go with you after I finish the sign."

"Yeah?"

"Yeah. We could be dealing with professional crooks,"

Tim said, repeating his earlier opinion. "And even if Biff Larson's behind all this, I don't think you should risk meeting him by yourself. He's probably still mean as ever."

Sandy thought Tim was overly cautious, but she watched him paint anyway.

"Looks great," she said when he finished. "Can we go now?"

Tim cleaned the brushes and put the paint away. Then they rode around to take down signs. By the time they had collected them all, their stomachs told them it was dinner time. They had seen no white pickup, even though they had biked past the TV repair shop again.

Sandy thought about the missing canary--and a missing horse--and a white pickup with a camper shell, one that seemed very hard to locate. *I wish Mr. Larson would get back from wherever he went*, she thought.

"What you doing tomorrow?" Tim asked.

"Family stuff. I think we're eating brunch with Uncle Jim and Aunt Marie. How about you?"

"I want to move my computer into the office. And get keys, so we can lock our office door," Tim said. "We'll be keeping files on our cases, and they have to be secret. Don't want anybody stealing them."

"A couple of weeks ago, I'd have said you were getting dramatic," Sandy said. "But with everything that's happened lately, I agree. I'll ask my dad if he can put a lock on our door."

It had been a long day. Toot and Sweet said goodnight.

8

"So you're in business now?" asked Aunt Marie. "What's it like being a detective?"

Sandy blushed. It was embarrassing to be put on the spot, with all her grown up family around her. "Kinda fun," she muttered, then asked, "Where's Muffy?"

Muffy was Aunt Marie's treasured Persian cat. She looked like one of those old muffs women wore when her grandmother was a girl. Nobody could wear one and hope to do anything. Wrists might as well be handcuffed. Then she had an idea. "Mom," she said, "I should be in the office, helping Tim get set up. He's moving his computer in, now that we have a desk."

"Well… ," her mother said, frowning. "We haven't even eaten yet. And we wanted to play bridge this afternoon."

Right, Sandy thought. *And I can twiddle my thumbs.*

Usually she found things to do while her parents enjoyed a card game with her aunt and uncle. She felt impatient today, though. She and Tim had things to talk over, plans to make. Maybe follow up on the idea of the gold mine.

"I can walk home," she said. "It's only about a mile."

Her mother said, "John, what do you think?"

Sandy was grateful to hear her father say, "Why not. She can eat, then head out. A little exercise is good for the Gophers' new pitcher."

Sandy gulped her brunch, ignoring desert. It was chocolate cake with ice cream. Her favorite food. But she was in too big a hurry to care. "Bye," she said, kissing Aunt Marie and hugging Uncle Jim. She was out the door and halfway down the block before anyone could call her back.

She ran, cutting through an alley behind the TV repair shop, the shortest way home. To her surprise, she saw the white pickup parked there. She was almost up to it, meaning to see if the sign were the magnetic kind, when she noticed someone in the driver's seat. *And he had seen her.*

"What you up to, kid?" the guy said in a gruff voice.

She didn't think she'd ever seen him before. If it had been Biff, she was pretty sure she'd recognize him. And he'd know her.

"Nothing," she said. "I just cut through here on my way home."

"And where would that be?" he wanted to know, but Sandy had already decided not to hang around in the alley. She ran like a shot, turning onto the street that would take her almost to her house. As she darted out of the alley, she heard the truck start, and wondered if he were planning to follow her. Alarmed, she thought, *If this guy has anything to do with our mystery, I don't want him to know where I live.* Instead of turning left on Grange

Avenue, she turned right and ran to the park. Dashing across the swing area, she came out in front of Mandy's home. Out of the corner of her eye, she thought she saw the pickup drive past as she ran up the steps. She didn't want him to see her knocking at the door, so she dashed around into the back yard. Mandy's pit bull growled and headed toward her. She knew the dog, but he wasn't the friendly kind. The potting shed, she thought in a panic. The door stood ajar. In a flash she was inside, banging the door closed. *What if the man heard the dog growling?* He'd know she didn't live here. Still, he wouldn't know *where* she lived.

What a bummer. Trapped in a shed, when she wanted to be in the office with Tim. Nobody was home here, she was almost sure, or someone would come out to see why the dog was raising such a ruckus.

She sat on a stool in the corner, wishing she at least had something to read. But practical Sandy had something to occupy her time, something new to think about. *It was a white pickup. He was a stranger. He wasn't tall and thin, though. I didn't get a really good look at him, but he might be about Biff's age. Was he in on the plot that*--in spite of Tim's comment that Biff was innocent until proven guilty, she still thought of Biff when she pondered the missing canary, and the missing horse. Those things had to be connected, she reasoned. She was almost sure it had something to do with the mine.

The dog was quiet now. Peering out the small window at the side of the shed, she saw him lying on the back patio. If she could just get over the fence before he noticed... .Quietly she opened the door. A ladder leaned against the apple tree behind the shed. She hurried up, then crawled along a sturdy branch to drop off into the neighbor's yard. *No dogs here*, she thought grate-fully. As she made her way out onto the street, she looked both ways. *No white pickup.* She could hardly wait to tell Tim what she had seen.

9

"Why is a stranger driving Larson's pickup?" was Tim's first comment. "Old man Larson *can't* be part of stealing a kid's pet and an old man's horse. He's honest. I'll bet on it."

"But *he's* out of town. Biff could have given the guy his keys." Sandy sat on one of the little chairs and breathed deeply. She had hurried home, and was still out of breath. "He didn't look like someone Mr. Larson would hire to help him. Nobody'd want that guy around."

"He *wasn't* tall?"

"Hard to say when he was sitting down. But he definitely wasn't thin. Beefy. And mean."

"Anybody'd look mean if he was chasing you in a pickup. You sure he was?"

"Tim." Sandy's look was enough to wilt an oak tree. "I

think our next step is to check at Ghost Town Flats, see if anybody up there saw Thunder."

"OK. But our folks won't let us go during the week," Tim objected.

"We'll have to tell them we want to go hiking in the mountains next Saturday."

"And they'll ask why we have to ride a bus to go on a hike." Tim was beginning to sound practical. "They'll tell us to walk up through the park"

"Think we could make it a school project?" Sandy wondered.

"Like a study of gold mining in the... ."

"The gold rush was fourth grade social studies," Sandy objected. "It's got to be something... ." She glanced at the computer. "That hooked up?"

"Sure. What you think I was doing while you were playing with Mandy's pit bull?"

Sandy ignored his teasing. "How about we look at one of those educational websites. Might get an idea for a report we'd be "required" to do before... ."

"No phone line, no internet." Tim snapped his fingers. "How about, 'Compare the grocery business in town with a remote store, say in a ghost town."

Sandy actually clapped her hands. "Right on," she said. "Not the title, maybe, but the project is perfect. Now, all we have to do is type out a page or two of ... ."

"How about we just make notes, like planning an outline?"

"Whatever." Sandy spun to glance around the office. "Now that's settled, what's left to do here?"

"Under control, fearless leader. All buttoned down."

"Then what say we bike over past the TV shop, see if the pickup's back in the alley?'

At the end of the block, Sandy turned back.

"Chicken out?" Tim asked, grinning.

"No, Sherlock. Just thought I'd change out of my Sunday best jeans and shirt. Don't want that geek to recognize me, if he's still there."

Tim agreed that wouldn't be cool. When she came back wearing shorts, a tee shirt, and a floppy hat, they headed toward the repair shop again, for what seemed like the twentieth time.

The truck was nowhere to be seen, either in the alley or in front of the store.

"Oh, well. Guess we'll have to put our investigation on hold," Sandy said. She felt relieved, in a way. Scrambling over fences was exciting, but she didn't want to do it again today.

10

Waiting wasn't something Toot and Sweet did well. Monday after school, they met in their office to write notes for the "report".

"Let's tell Mom now," Sandy said, as she and Tim prepared for their Saturday "interview" with the man who owned Ghost Town General Store. "We'll say we're going to talk to Mr. Grover, too."

"How do you know Mr. Mason will be available this weekend?" Mrs. Carpenter asked when they found her in the kitchen. "You'd better call. Make an appointment."

Sandy looked at Tim as if to say, *Parents!* But she picked up the phone book, looked up a number, and called. "All set," she said when she put the phone down. "We can take the bus up. There's prob'ly only one right now, until fishing season really gets going on Lake Bremer."

"That won't be necessary," Mrs. Carpenter advised the detectives. "I'll drive you."

"That's OK," Tim said. "We don't want to bother you."

"No bother," Sandy's mother assured them. "School work's important."

Toot and Sweet stared at each other, trying to hide their dismay. Their shoulders drooped as they went back to their office.

"We gotta think of something," Sandy groaned. "It won't do any good at all if she takes us up there."

"Yeah." Tim sat at his computer, touching the keys as if they would provide a magical answer.

"Now that we've told her we have a report to do, we'll *have* to do it," Sandy said. "How can we *ever* get to the mine?"

Nothing had suggested a way out of their dilemma on Tuesday when Sandy went to baseball practice. She was a few minutes early, and decided to ask Coach Peterson more about Biff.

"That boy loved baseball. Fact, it was about all he lived for," Coach said.

"Did he pitch for the Gophers?"

"Started out, but he couldn't keep his grades up." He went on to explain that, while Biff was in elementary school, he barely squeaked through. "But when he went on to high school after eighth grade, he hit a real slump. Didn't study at all, according to Coach Wellborn. When he failed for a full semester, Wellborn had to drop him from all sports. School's pretty strict about that."

Unlike Exeter and Middleton, both larger communities, Gainsburg did not have an intermediate school. Kids went to elementary until they graduated from eighth grade.

"And I guess he wasn't eligible to play in the summer?"

"No. The town backs the school on the grades thing."

"Think that explains why he set off the alarm? And called about the bomb?"

"I'm sure of it. He must have thought he was getting even by stealing equipment," Coach said. "He created a lot of problems, all through school. But I never felt he was a really bad kid."

When they met Thursday after school on Sandy's front porch, the detectives had begun to feel desperate.

"What can we do?" Tim asked, a frown creasing his forehead.

"Not a clue," Sandy said, her frown matching her partners.

Then Aunt Marie stopped by, and the problem was solved. She asked Mrs. Carpenter to drive her to Exeter.

"Jim's taking the truck," she explained. "And I need to get material from that yardage shop. For the new curtains."

"I promised the kids I'd drive them up the mountain." Mrs. Carpenter sighed.

"It's OK," Sandy assured her mother, trying not to let relief show in her face.

"Bus is sort of fun," Tim said. "And we'll have time to hike after the interview."

"Buses are not fun if you have to ride them often," Aunt Marie said. "But thanks, kids. I'm trying to get the living room redecorated before my cousins come from New Jersey."

Even in the office, Toot and Sweet controlled their delight. Turning cartwheels might call too much attention to their proposed trip. Questions might be asked, and the real reason, their investigation into the old mine, might be discovered.

"We're big enough to hike to the mine on our own," Sandy said. "Parents should get that 'little kid' thing out of their minds."

Now that their plans could go ahead, they biked to the bus depot to see if they had to make reservations.

"No, it's first come, first served," the woman behind the desk told them. "And the busy season starts about the time school's out. Three weeks yet. No reason to think you can't get on the Saturday bus."

Tickets, they learned, would be $7.50 round trip. Fifteen dollars would wipe out their budget. In fact, they'd have to use part of their allowance, too.

"Maybe we can charge Mrs. Barnes expenses. Even Encyclopedia Brown did that," Sandy said.

"We can ask, but maybe *after* we solve the case."

Biking home, even conservative Tim was doing wheelies.

11

Neither detective said anything as they boarded the bus on Saturday. Not, that is, until the streets of Gainsburg were left behind. As the bus began its climb up the mountain, they looked at each other and each whispered an excited "Hey." They had talked about the importance of not letting anyone overhear their plans.

"We don't know *who* might be part of the scheme," Tim had said.

They talked about the interview they'd be doing, then about the hike into the hills.

"Return bus doesn't leave Ghost Town until four," Sandy remembered. "We'll have plenty of time to eat our lunch, then do some exploring."

"Be fun," Tim agreed. "I haven't been up here since Dad

took me fishing, and that meant sitting by the dumb lake dodg-
ing mosquitoes." Fishing, like any sport, wasn't Tim's idea of a
way to spend a day.

"You aren't going to complain all day, are you?" Sandy
knew her partner wouldn't choose to hike either, unless it had
something to do with a mystery.

When the bus pulled to a stop in front of the general store,
Tim and Sandy were the only passengers getting off. A family
with two small kids was going on to the lake, they guessed, and
they had heard several fishermen talk of the boat they would be
renting.

As they climbed down the steps, Sandy said, "We have to
talk to Mr. Mason. He's expecting us."

"Right," Tim said, pulling a small notebook out of his
pocket. "I'll take notes on what he says. Gotta make this look like
the real Patoot."

Entering the store, they found the owner behind a counter
laden with candy bars, a jar of pickled eggs, maps of the lake area,
fishing lures and racks of potato chips. They learned that business
in this remote store was slow all winter, that Mr. Mason considered closing and going to Florida next year from October on.

"But I'll always be here when a fisherman wants to buy a
can of worms, or food for a picnic lunch." He grinned at them,
showing how much he enjoyed his business. "And you'd be surprised," he continued, "how often I sell a few yards of dress material or a hammer to the families that live nearby." There were four
or five homes not far from the store, people who would do their
regular shopping here instead of driving down to Gainsburg.

When he had shown them the barrel of dill pickles, the
stone crock of sauerkraut, cans of beans, screw drivers, nails and
hammers, and a limited selection of fabrics, they all went outside.

"Guess the main difference is your slow season," Tim said. "And you've got a lot of stuff they don't have down at Grover's."

"We're comparing your store with business down in Gainsburg," Sandy told Mr. Mason. "That's what this report is about."

They thanked him, and lingered on the porch for a few minutes before dashing off on the trail.

"You have a long wait for the return bus," the man said. "Think you'll be needing anything for lunch?"

"We brought some stuff," Tim said, pointing to his bulging pockets.

"We're going to hike for a while. Don't get a chance too often," Sandy said.

"Good. That means I won't be letting you down if I close early. Bus comes by at four, but lately nobody has come to buy after about one o'clock on Saturday. I don't mind sitting in a rocking chair on the porch, but it gets boring after a while."

"Guess it would," Sandy said. "We'll find plenty to do. Don't worry about us."

As they hiked off in the direction of the haunted mine, Sandy turned to look at Mr. Mason, almost hidden behind his newspaper. "We don't need any help," she asserted, as if trying to reassure herself.

12

They had decided not to ask the man about Thunder. They were sure to see signs if the horse had been brought up here.

"Think these guys are trying to get gold out of the mine?" Tim asked.

"If that's their scheme, they have a lot of hard work ahead of them. But it would explain the need for a canary." Sandy's ankle twisted as she slipped on a rock. "Ouch," she said, and stopped to rub it for a couple of minutes, sitting on a boulder beside the trail.

"You OK?" Tim asked. He sat on a fallen log and glanced around. "Rough going," he said, kicking at a rock. Sandy agreed, still rubbing her ankle.

"Think we'll see the old cabin where the miner lived? You know, the one that turned up missing," Tim stood to look around. When Sandy got up, he asked, "Sure you're OK to walk again?"

She tested her ankle by stepping forward on it. "Yeah. I'm good to go."

The way was rocky. More than once they found themselves scrambling to keep their balance. Though they were impatient, running was not practical.

"Gotta be careful, or we'll both end up with bunged ankles," Tim observed as he stepped around a log that had fallen across the trail.

"Hard to tell if a horse came this way," Sandy said, "but they'd need one to get supplies to the mine." She squinted against the sun, then glanced down to watch where she was stepping. She grabbed Tim's arm. "That proves it," she said. "A horse, for sure." In the path ahead was a pile of horse manure.

"If they expected anyone to come by this way, they'd have shoved that off the trail," Tim said. "But these guys aren't long in the thinking department. Who in his right mind would try to dig gold out of an abandoned mine? Nuggets aren't going to be lying around, just for the taking."

"You have a point," Sandy said. "Getting ore processed must be hard. Cost a bundle, too, you'd think. But who cares? All I want is to get Billy's canary back."

"And maybe Thunder."

Lowering her voice, Sandy said, "We'd better keep as quiet as possible."

"Right," Tim said in a whisper.

They walked on. Some time later, they saw a cabin to the side of the trail. They approached cautiously, slipping from the cover of one tree to the next. When they were close, they saw someone through the open door.

"That's him," Sandy whispered. "The one who chased me in the pickup."

"Looks like he could be about Biff's age," Tim whispered back. "And mean, like you said. Hefty, too. Wouldn't want to meet up with his muscles."

The man came out. They backed away as cautiously as they had approached. He went around to the rear of the cabin. They heard a horse whinny. Tim and Sandy ducked behind a huge boulder, holding their breath. They did not relax until he rode past.

"See, he's going to the mine," Sandy whispered. "At least he's got a bunch of tools, like shovels and pickaxes, stuff they'd be likely to use down there. "

"Can't be far," Tim said. "We gotta be really careful, though."

Sandy put a finger to her lips, nodding toward the trail. "We can stay in among the trees," she said.

"That had to be Thunder, don't you think?" Tim asked.

"Thunder didn't have that white spot on his chest," Sandy said. "But I guess they could have painted it on to disguise him." Then, " We'd better not talk any more. We don't know how many there are, and we'd be in trouble if anyone heard us."

They slipped slowly from tree to tree, turning often to make sure they weren't being followed. Then, quite suddenly, they saw the entrance to the mine. Rocks had fallen over the tracks that had once carried a miner's cart down to where the actual mining took place. The horse--Sandy was almost positive it was Thunder from the proud lift of his head--was tied to a sapling. What had once been a clearing was filled with scrub brush and young trees. Sandy reached out to take Tim's hand. She pointed. In one of the bushes hung the canary's cage, covered by someone's shirt. *They were smart enough to keep it covered,* she thought. *Too much sun couldn't be healthy for a canary.*

The man they had followed was unloading tools from the saddle, untying ropes, calling, "Give us a hand, Larry."

Another man stepped out, blinking in the sunlight.

"Yeah, Butch. You got all the stuff?"

"Everything they had at that store. You check out the tunnel?"

"I'm not going in there by myself. The place is haunted. Everybody knows that," Larry said. "They closed the mine after the cave- in that trapped those guys." He went on. "They tried to rescue the men, according to what I read. Finally gave up. Said they were dead, no sense risking any more lives."

"Hell of a thing, having a mountain fall in on you." Butch picked up some tools, saying, "Let's get with it. No sense standin' around all day."

"Listen, jerk. It happened before. And you and your dad almost got trapped."

Butch snapped, "Look. I let you guys know the risks up front. Don't mention this in front of Biff any more. He's startin' t' freak."

"Not the risks that bug him. He's scared spitless of ghosts. You remember the dreams he told us about seeing his mother, back from the dead."

"Where is the wimp, anyway?" Butch asked.

"Somewhere around, I guess."

"Well, let's find him. We gotta get the show on the road."

"You positive the money's hid in there?"

"I was with my dad when he buried it. See, his partner wanted his share. I heard them arguing one night, yellin' at each other. The other guy insisted on a split. That was when Dad decided better t' work alone."

"So did they... ?"

"Yeah. Dad figured no sense fightin' it out with the idiot. If Mullins got caught spending part of the loot, nothing tied them together. I tagged along when Dad stashed his share up here. He should 'a let me work with him after that, sort of cover his back." Butch snorted. "Workin' alone, he got caught in less than a month. He's back in jail."

Larry looked baffled. "What makes you think it's time to get the money out? Your dad tell you to come get it?"

"You kiddin'? He'd skin me alive if he knew what I was up to."

Hidden by the trees, Tim and Sandy exchanged glances. Now they knew the real reason why the canary and the horse had been stolen. They watched as the two carried pickaxes to the mine entrance, then came back for shovels and other equipment.

Larry picked up a canteen, shook it, and said, "I forgot to fill this. Where'd you say to find the spring?"

Butch waved a hand. "Down there," he said. Larry disappeared down a winding path, saying, "Be back in a minute."

"Spring ain't that close," Butch snorted. He glanced around and started into the cave-like darkness, then shook his head. "Could be Larry's right," he said. "No sense working by myself."

As Tim edged toward the canary, he kicked loose a rock. The sound seemed dangerously loud in the quiet mountain air.

"What was that?" Butch asked himself, peering over his shoulder, then walking in the direction of the noise.

Sandy could see Tim's eyes, round with fear. He remained frozen where he stood. She dropped back out of sight, just as Butch came around a boulder and saw Tim.

"What you doin' here, punk?" he demanded.

Tim's mouth moved, but no words came out.

"What you doin?" the man repeated. "Who's with you."

"N-n-n-no-b-b-body," Tim managed through stiff lips.

Butch dragged Tim toward the mine. "You got a buddy out here? Anybody else sneaking around?"

Tim said in a shaky voice, "I-I-I w-was with some scouts, out there." He waved in the general direction of the trail. "They w-w-went down the side of that canyon. I started, but it looked too steep. I got s-s-scared."

"Don't want nobody poking around out here," Butch said in a surly voice.

"I w-w-won't tell anybody," Tim stammered.

"Best we make sure you don't," Butch snarled, reaching for rope that lay where he had dropped it. He looped it around Tim's hands, then tied him to a tree.

Tim seemed petrified. He hadn't even tried to get away. At that moment a rock came hurtling from behind a nearby tree, clipping Butch on the head. He sank to the ground with a grunt, and lay quietly at Tim's feet. Just as she saw Tim grin with relief, Sandy heard a voice behind her.

"Nice pitch."

Turning, Sandy gasped as she recognized Biff Larson not three feet away from her.

13

Overwhelmed with the complications to Butch's plan, Biff thought, *If the guys get wise to a kid up here, who knows what they'll do to her. I know Butch. Nothin' gets in his way.*

"You best come with me," he said, grabbing Sandy's arm and pulling her in the direction of the cabin. "What you doin' up here, anyway?"

"I'm investigating the disappearance of Billy's canary. And Mr. Melvin's horse."

He stared at her.

"I'm a detective," she explained. "I'm not going to try to run away. You can let go my arm."

"Hey. I read about you. Right on the front page."

Biff didn't want to stand around outside talking things over. He led her into the cabin, then dropped her arm. "So what gave you the idea to come snoopin' around here?"

"I knew miners used canaries to test oxygen in a mine. Since the canary disappeared, cage and all, this seemed the logical place to look for him."

"Hmmm. Smart kid. How'd you learn to think like that?"

"Reading mysteries, I guess. Besides baseball, that's my biggest interest."

"Baseball? I used to play."

"I know," Sandy said. "You were the talk of the town, Biff. Someone I always looked up to. I'm a pitcher, too."

Biff, ill at ease that she knew his identity, grunted, "What makes you think that's my name?"

"I've been talking with the coach about you."

Biff started to grin. "Peterson?"

"Yeah. Coach Peterson. Told me I had *almost* as good an arm as you, when you were in eighth grade."

"He did?" Biff sat on one of the rough benches near the door. "You playin' for the Gophers?" he asked abruptly.

"Yep. My first season as a pitcher," she told him. "Bet Coach Peterson'd like to see you show up. Maybe he could get you on the Seniors."

He looked eager for a moment. Then his face settled into a frown. "Naw. I dropped out when I was a junior. No grades. Then that trip t' juvenile hall… ."

"You could sign up for summer school. Bet you could get good grades now that you're… ." Sandy stopped, holding her breath. There was a noise at the door.

"What the… ?" Biff said, turning toward the door as it creaked opened.

14

When a scruffy looking dog nosed his way in, Biff let out his breath, swore, and said, "That danged door. Won't stay closed." Then he reached out a hand and said, "Here, Brother. Good boy."

Brother? Biff's got a dog named Brother? Sandy shook her head in amazement. This guy was full of surprises.

" 'Spect you're hungry, pooch," he said, his freckled face relaxing into a friendly grin. The young man reached toward the dirty dishes stacked in a basin on a makeshift cupboard. "Only thing left's a bone, but you like chewin'." The dog sat at his feet and began chomping the gristle left on the bone. Biff said, "I p'robly ought to go over 't the store and get more grub."

Sandy remembered the sandwich she still had in her pocket. Pulling it out, she reached it toward Biff. "Pretty scrunched," she said, "but it's ham. You might like it. Brother, too."

Biff stared at her as if an offer of kindness from anyone was beyond his understanding.

"Go on. You're prob'ly hungry, too."

He didn't move to accept her offer. Instead he scratched his head and muttered, "Nobody does anything for Biff. Good ole Biff, they figure. He can look out for himself." A mean look crossed his face and he glared at her.

Not knowing what else to do, Sandy pulled the ham out of half the sandwich and reached it down to the dog. "Nice Brother," she said. Her generous gesture seemed to impress Biff. She nibbled at part of the bread, saving the other half sandwich. She was half afraid to offer it to this strange young man but wished he would take it. When he didn't, she wrapped it back in its foil and put it on the cupboard beside dishes that looked as though they had never been washed. Neatness wasn't really her thing, but she almost wished there were water and soap to scrub them.

"Will you think about going back to school?" she asked.

Biff snorted. "Nobody wants t' see *me* comin' back."

"I think you're wrong. Coach Peterson sounded like he'd... ."

Biff interrupted. "Wellborn still coaching high school? He'd boot my... ." He broke off, as if biting the words that might spill out of his mouth.

"Why don't you talk to Coach--Peterson, that is. He'd put in a good word for you."

Biff's face softened. "Yeah, Peterson. He was pretty nice to me. Tough, though."

He made me study."

"He could do it again, if you'd let him. Give it a try.
Maybe he teaches summer school. And there's the test you can
take, gets you the same as a high school diploma."

"He--eck. I dropped out in eleventh grade."

"So? Get a tutor. Bet my mom would help you." Sandy
was growing impatient. "Look, you seem to like animals. You
should know they want to be with their owners. That canary
belongs to Billy Barnes."

Biff shook himself, as if rousing from a dream. "Canary?"

"The one you took. Were you planning to use it down in
the mine? Don't you think it's got rights? Did you ever stop to
think what stealing it did to a really nice little kid?"

The young man stared at her for several minutes before
saying, "OK. **Okay**. Maybe I'll get it back. Don't care much for
Butch's plan anyway. Another cave-in might happen when we
went down. And I don't want to be tied in with a... ." He broke
off. Sandy was sure he didn't want to spill a secret. He couldn't
know she and Tim had heard the real reason those three were at
the mine. At least, she didn't think he'd been standing behind her
before she threw her knockout pitch.

"Whose idea was this, anyway," she asked. If he wasn't
saying anything about the old bank robbery, she didn't want to
risk it either. She didn't want to make him uncomfortable when
he was about to become helpful. She pictured Billy's face when he
saw his bird again, and mentally crossed her fingers. And
Thunder? If Biff agreed, he could be returned too.

"Some guy. You wouldn't know him. Be hard to get
around him, though."

"The mean one? He might still be knocked out."

"Yeah?" Biff stared at her, disbelieving.

"I pitched that rock at him. Saw him drop just before you... ."

"Oh, yeah." He frowned. "So you want me to double-cross a buddy?"

"Is he really a buddy? Would he back you up in a tight spot?"

"Well... ." Biff looked at her uncertainly and reached down to pet Brother.

"Billy really misses his canary," Sandy said, her face sad at the thought.

"Come to think of it," Biff said, "Butch was about to let Larry and me hold the bag on that holdup. Almost weaseled out. Yeah, I guess it's time to take the canary back."

He started toward the door, then turned and pointed to the dog. "Stay," he said. As an afterthought, he added, "You stay with him, whatever your name is. Just to be sure he doesn't wander off."

Sandy started to argue, then thought she might be better able to help if she stayed in the background. She watched the door close after him and reached out a hand to the dog. "Biff," she said thoughtfully. "Not so bad after all, is he?"

15

Biff had been gone only a short time when Sandy heard voices. Looking around for a place to hide, she scrunched behind the rough bed in the corner of the room. What she saw when the door opened made her gasp. Tim stood in the doorway, the canary cage in his hand.

"Sandy," he called. "Come out, come out, wherever you are."

"Don't be a goon," she said sharply. "Did Biff give you the canary? Did he say we could leave?"

Before Tim could explain, Sandy heard the sound of a horse whinnying. "Is that Thunder?" she asked.

Without a word, Tim handed her the cage, picked up the dog and went back out. She followed. There, holding Thunder's lead rein, stood Biff. "Get on," he told them. "We gotta move it.

Now."

"The mean one?"

"Still out cold," Tim said. "The other guy didn't come back yet."

She stared at him, unable to take it all in. Biff glared at her.

"Come on, kid. Get with it. You and him--." He motioned toward Tim. "You two ride. I'll lead the horse."

Sandy didn't ask any more questions. Climbing on a rock near Thunder, she hoisted herself up, then leaned over to take the cage from Tim. Reaching her free hand down, she helped him up behind her. They had ridden the big black horse for fun before, but this time it was serious. Biff whistled to the dog to follow. Tugging at the lead rein, he headed toward the main trail back to Ghost Town Flats. No one spoke. There wasn't much to say, and no one wanted to be heard by the two who remained at the mine.

When the store was in sight, Sandy breathed a sigh of relief. A lot of thoughts had gone on under her baseball cap. She was glad to be on the way home with Billy's canary. As they stopped in front of the store, she pointed and said, "Look. It feels as if we've been gone a week, but there's the bus coming now. It must be about four o'clock."

"You ridin' the bus back to town?" Biff wanted to know.

"Right. You need a way to get down the mountain, and three on Thunder would be too many."

Tim looked a trifle disappointed as he slid off the big horse's back.

Sandy said, "Won't Billy be surprised?"

"Gosh, you're right. We get to take his Twinby back." Tim grinned. "And think what our folks will say when they hear what Toot and Sweet have accomplished today."

As they climbed onto the bus, Sandy waved to Biff. "See you in town," she said.

Settling the cage at her feet, Sandy leaned back in her seat and sighed. What a day it had been. Glancing at Tim, she saw his eyes had already closed. *Not a bad idea*, she thought as she, too, drifted into sleep.

16

Biff rode down the mountain, Brother following. "Road sure is easier than ridin' through the brush," he commented to himself as the horse loped along. He wondered what Butch and Larry were doing. He wondered if Butch needed a doctor, and felt a little guilty about leaving him that way. But he'd never have been able to get the kids and the animals out if he'd waited to help his former buddies. It was sort of like trying to decide whether to help the "good guys" or the crooks. Butch did seem headed for a life of crime. What he was trying up there amounted to stealing from his own father. Granted, it was stolen money, but... .

He wondered if that girl could be right. Was it possible that, with Peterson's help, he could go back to school. And get into baseball again? His dad would like it if he got involved in studying again. Maybe he'd like the baseball angle, too.

When I was a kid, seemed like no matter what I did, he didn't like it. Wonder if he's back yet. Sure was funny, him saying it was OK for the guys to stay at the shop. I never got a feel for what he was thinking. He didn't seem mad, though. Kind of sorry, in fact, about his havin' to leave right after I got there.

As he neared the farm where Thunder had been stolen, he gulped down his fears and decided to tell the old farmer the truth. But Mr. Melvin wasn't there. Biff rode the horse into the barn and put him in one of the stalls. He hunted around for oats, and filled a bucket with water for Thunder as well. Seeing the currycomb on the wall in the stable, he scrubbed the white spot Butch had insisted on painting onto Thunder's chest. Not all of it came off, even when he dipped the comb into water. He gave up after a few tries, saying, "He'll be glad t' see his horse again. Maybe won't notice this too much." He rubbed Thunder's nose and said, "I'll be missing you, old friend. Maybe I can rent a ride on you now and then."

He hurried away. Now that Thunder was returned to his rightful owner, Biff didn't really want to talk about how he came up missing. The more he could forget about Butch, the better. Larry might shape up. If he got away from Butch. Who knew what that guy was likely to do? Walking toward the room he had shared with the other two behind the TV repair shop, he wondered if his dad was back from the business trip. Seeing the old Thunderbird parked in front of the shop, he hesitated, then shook his head and said, "Cold feet won't help none."

Inside, he noted with relief that Mr. Larson was alone. "Dad," he began, not even giving his father a chance to greet him. "I gotta tell you something." Before he could stop, the whole story of Butch's plan, and his part in it, had spilled out. "I should've told you these guys are the ones--that convenience store robbery, y' know, the reason I got sent back. I'll leave if you want me to. Guess I haven't been much good to you."

"Son," Mr. Larson said, reaching out to hug Biff. "It takes a man to own up when he's wrong. You're back now. That's all I care about."

They stood facing each other. Neither spoke for some time. Then Mr. Larson broke the silence. "I sort of hoped you might want to work here with me. This business can be yours when I get ready to retire."

"Family business?" Biff grinned. "There's something else I'd like to do, too. There was this kid up in the mountain made a suggestion." And he blurted out Sandy's idea that he go back to school. "She thought Coach Peterson might get me back into pitching, if I keep my grades up."

"Who is this girl?" Mr. Larson asked.

"I never got her name."

"What on earth was a kid doing up near the mine?"

"She and her buddy were looking for the canary."

"A canary?"

"Yeah. The one I took so's Butch could go--I guess we were all supposed to help dig out the loot. I think he said it was the third level down. The stolen bank money."

"How old is this girl?"

"Just a kid. Maybe in eighth grade. But she's some pitcher. She knocked Butch out with a rock," Biff said. "That's how we managed to get away without any trouble."

"Peterson'll know who she is. We'll call him." Mr. Larson seemed to be trying to swallow a lump in his throat. "I love you, son. Together, we'll turn your life around."

It was Biff's turn to gulp. "I didn't know you even liked me." He rubbed his eyes, sniffling a little.

"Son, I've always loved you. Just wasn't any good at show-ing it."

17

Tim and Sandy awoke when the bus pulled in at the station. They looked at each other and, in one voice, said, "Billy."

"I can hardly wait to see his face," Sandy said.

"Wish we had our bikes," Tim complained.

Walking to their neighborhood, they took turns carrying the cage. After all that had happened, their feet dragged even though they were in a hurry to see Billy. As if the canary sensed it was going home it sang, something it didn't usually do when the cage was covered.

"Poor bird. We're lucky it's still alive," Sandy said.

Passing the Carpenter house, they saw no car in the driveway. "Guess Mom's still in Exeter, or over at Aunt Marie's. It was hard to realize she had waved goodbye to her mother and aunt just this morning. It seemed more like a month ago.

They walked past Tim's home and started up the steps at the Barnes place when Billy came dashing out. "You found him. You found Twinby," he shouted. "Mom, they've got my birdie."

Mrs. Barnes came to the door. "I don't know what to say," she began. "I didn't want to even think it, but I was afraid the bird was gone for good." She reached out to take the cage. "You are two *very* good detectives." She seemed overwhelmed.

Embarrassed, Tim looked down at his shoes. Sandy smiled and said, "We didn't want Billy to be disappointed. We weren't about to give up."

"This calls for a celebration," Mrs. Barnes insisted. "We'll have a 'Welcome Home Twinby party'."

A voice called from the neighboring porch. "What's this all about?"

Turning, Tim saw his father. He started to say something, but Mrs. Barnes interrupted. "These detectives have found Billy's canary. Aren't they wonderful!" Glancing down, she saw that Billy had opened the cage and was reaching in for his bird. "Not out here, son," she cautioned. "We don't want him to fly away."

Billy quickly closed the cage.

"We can put him up on his stand," Mrs. Barnes said. "But we'll keep it away from the window from now on."

Tim ran to his house, shouting, "Dad. We've got to get together with Sandy's folks. We have a bunch of things to tell you all."

Mrs. Barnes called out, "Maybe we can all have dinner here. Billy's dad and I want to hear the whole story, too."

Just then Mrs. Carpenter turned into their driveway. Sandy dashed to greet her.

"Where's Dad?" she asked.

"At the gym, but he should be home soon."

Sandy blurted out, "We got Billy's canary. And Thunder. And there's more."

After a big hug, Mrs. Carpenter stepped back to take a good look at her daughter. "Looks like you could use a shower and a change of clothes."

"I do feel kind of grungy," Sandy admitted.

When she came out of the shower, her father was sitting in his chair but for once he wasn't hidden behind a newspaper. He said, "Well, super-sleuth, I hear you and Tim found Billy's canary."

The phone rang, and he reached to answer it. Sandy heard him say, "Pizza? To welcome Twinby home? OK. We'll be right over."

18

When Larry came up from the spring, he found Butch lying motionless where he had fallen.

"What gives?" he wondered out loud. Kneeling by the still figure, he checked for a pulse, relieved when he felt an unsteady beat. Butch groaned. Larry turned him onto his back and examined the bruised spot on his temple.

"Holy cow. What hit you?"

"O-o-o-o-oh. My head," Butch groaned.

"Biff do this?" Larry asked.

"I don't think so. There was this kid. I was tying him up and, all of a sudden--Pow. I don't know what hit me."

"I'd better get you to a doctor. But how? The horse is gone. Think that kid took him?" Reaching down, he helped Butch to his feet. "You're gonna have t' help me out. Can't carry you all the way to that store."

With Larry's arm around his waist, Butch managed to stagger along beside him. It was a slow go. "Come on," Larry urged from time to time. As they approached the cabin, Larry made a decision. "Better put you to bed in there. My guess is you have a concussion. I can make it out, call a doctor from that pay phone by the store. Be faster in the long run."

Opening the cabin door, he added, "Biff can take care of you until I get back with some help." But Biff was not in the cabin. Larry eased Butch onto the bed, then hurried out. The rough trail slowed him down, but he arrived at the store about forty minutes later. Checking the directory, he found a doctor listed in the Ghost Town area, with the information he was available only in the summer, and only for emergencies. Vacationing? Larry wondered at a practice that allowed a doctor to spend months away from it. Dialing, he was relieved when a voice said, "Yes?"

Explaining the problem, Larry asked, "Can you come to the cabin?"

"I'll do better than that," the doctor said. "My son has a horse you can use to bring your friend out. He'll probably need to go to the hospital. I'll arrange for an ambulance to take him down to Exeter."

Larry was given directions to Dr. Barry's house, where a horse was already saddled. The doctor's son had readily agreed to loan the horse when he learned why it was needed.

Riding to the cabin was easier. When Larry succeeded in getting the semi-conscious Butch into the saddle, he led the animal and its complaining burden out to Ghost Town Flats.

As good as his promise, the doctor was waiting with an ambulance. In response to Larry's question, he explained, "My

partner and I have an agreement. I get to summer in the mountains. He spends three winter months in Florida."

By this time, the attendant had the patient settled in the
ambulance. Dr. Barry got in beside Butch. No siren was turned
on. Traffic in the mountains was so sparse it was probably not
necessary. *And*, Larry reflected, *it seems wrong, somehow, to
disturb the quiet of the mountainside.*

Staring after the departing vehicle, Larry said to himself,
"Now I think I'll put a few miles between me and this place. No
telling what Biff's up to. If he's covering his own tail by ratting on
us, I don't want to be anywhere around."

As he stood by the road considering how best to disappear,
a car came up from the lake. A fisherman, he guessed. Putting
out a thumb he made the familiar "Going my way?" sign and was
relieved when the driver pulled over.

"Funny place to be hitching," one of the men said.

"My buddy had an accident while we were hiking up here.
Dr. Barry took him to the hospital. In Exeter, I think he said."

"Yeah. That's where they'd go," the man agreed. "And you
missed the bus?"

"Where you heading?" Larry asked, to change the subject.

"We drove up from Boulder Creek, over by Cranden," the
driver said.

"I'd sure appreciate if I could ride that far with you," Larry
said. "We were staying somewhere around there. I'd like to get
back and pick up our stuff."

He stayed quiet during the ride, listening now and then to
fish stories the men told. He'd be on a bus to somewhere pretty
soon. He'd had enough of Butch's nutty schemes, he decided.
*Dumb to even get involved with him again after that last stunt.
Robbing a convenience store? I'd better pick my friends more*

carefully, he thought. He'd have been long gone if he hadn't taken time to get medical attention for the guy. But he admitted he couldn't leave anyone in Butch's predicament. This way, he could sleep tonight, no matter where he stopped.

19

Six parents beamed at their children. Mr. and Mrs. Barnes were delighted to see Billy happy again. Mr. and Mrs. Jared were relieved that Tim had returned safely. Mr. and Mrs. Carpenter were obviously trying not to preach to Sandy, though her mother did say, "Never again, Sandy. We can't have you in that kind of danger." The parents were all proud of the new detectives, but agreed their investigations should be limited to things like lost library books.

"You two are full of surprises," Mr. Jared said.

"And curiosity," Sandy's mother added, looking somewhat shaken. "It's likely to lead you into more trouble. You know the saying, 'Curiosity killed the cat'."

"Just what I was thinking," Mrs. Barnes said. "They risked a lot to get Billy's canary back."

Billy just took a giant bite of pizza, smiling around it.

Toot and Sweet mentioned they had overheard something about a bank robbery. "An old one, from the sound of things," Sandy said.

"Maybe the one in Cranden about five years ago," Tim suggested.

"How do you know about that?" his mother asked. "You were only nine at the time."

"I read," he said, as if that explained everything.

"We thought we'd go back up and see if we can find the stolen money," Sandy said.

"That's a job for the police," her father insisted. The other adults agreed. With some reluctance, Tim and Sandy agreed to call the authorities. "Right after dinner," Sandy promised. "But can't we go up when they dig it out?"

"We'll see," said her father. Her mother just frowned.

The phone was ringing when the Carpenters walked into their house. Sandy's call to the police was postponed. Her father picked up the phone, and in a moment handed it to Sandy. "Another satisfied customer," was all he said.

"Hello," Sandy said, wondering who it might be. The people most concerned with their case had all been at the Barnes' home, or so she thought.

"Young lady, I have to thank you How did you do it?"

"Do what?" Sandy asked, thoroughly confused. Who could this be?

"You *are* Sandy Carpenter?"

"Yes," she said. She still didn't recognize the voice.

"Right. You and your friend found the little boy when he came to see Thunder?"

"Yes. He was pretty bummed out when Thunder

wasn't there."

"Tell the kid he can come and ride for free. Thunder's back in the stable, and I can guess you had something to do with it."

"Mr. Melvin?"

"That's me."

"It's true Tim and I found him. But Biff Larson was the one who brought him back to you."

"Old man Larson's son?"

"That's the one."

"What did he have to do with it?"

"He's the one who actually put Thunder back in the stable." There was no need, Sandy reasoned, to tell him Biff had been in on taking Thunder away. Best if everybody in town started thinking of Biff in a different way. *No more juvie for Biff,* she thought with satisfaction.

When she got off the phone, Sandy turned to her mother and started to ask, "Do you think...?" when the phone interrupted her. Reaching to answer, she said "This is the Carpenter residence." Her face broke into a smile when she heard a man say, "Are you the young lady I have to thank for sending Biff home?"

"Uh--uh--. Did he say that?"

"What he told me leads me to believe you've given my boy back to me. I don't have words to thank you."

"Is he going to school again?"

"He said you thought Coach Peterson might be willing to get him in again, and help him become eligible to pitch for the Senior Gophers. What kind of magic do you work?"

"Coach said he was a good kid. All I did was make a suggestion."

"And Biff took it. That's what seems so like a miracle to me. I love that boy. And I think he knows it now." Mr. Larson cleared his throat and added, "He's told me he wants to turn his life around. He started by making a police report. The cops want to meet with everyone involved."

Replacing the phone, Sandy realized how tired she was. Just then the phone rang again. She sighed and asked her mother, "Can you get that?"

Mrs. Carpenter picked it up and said, "Carpenter residence." A few minutes later she hung up and said, "The police will want to take a formal report tomorrow."

20

At the police station the following day, Sandy and Tim went with Biff to Chief Shaw's office. To their surprise, the tall thin man was sitting beside his desk. The chief introduced them, saying, "This is Detective Burns from the Cranden Police Department. He's been looking into a bank robbery that happened in their precinct about five years ago."

Sandy started to say something, glanced at Tim and decided not to say, *And we thought he was one of the thieves.* She almost asked, Why did you want to buy nails at the hardware store that day? *Let it go*, she told herself. *Probably just his cover.*

"These two," the chief went on, indicating Sandy and Tim, "are our newest detectives. They're pretty good at solving difficult cases."

Sandy said, "Biff can tell you more about the stolen

money than we can. We were only investigating the disappearance of Twinby and Thunder."

"He gave us most of the details on the phone last night," Chief Shaw said. "Now about this 'Butch'. We'd like to locate him."

"Last time I saw him was when I collected the canary and the horse--and Tim. He was knocked out at the time. Didn't I tell you that?" Biff said.

"Someone went up there early this morning to check. No sign of him anywhere."

"Maybe he came to. Larry would have found him anyway. I guess he'd hang with the program."

"Smith, the guy we sent up, said there were picks and shovels at the mine entrance. A canteen filled with water. Nobody around, he said."

"Think Larry got a doctor for him?" Tim asked.

Sandy chimed in, "There's a doctor who practices during the summer in Ghost Town Flats. Larry might have gotten in touch with him. I hit Butch pretty hard with that rock."

When the chief gave her a questioning glance she explained. "I pitch on the school team. Didn't expect to do any pitching up at the mine, but he looked mean. And he was threatening Tim."

"He *is* mean," Biff commented. "That's why I didn't feel too bad about leaving him up there."

The chief put in a call to the doctor in the mountain community. Advised that Butch had been taken to Exeter Hospital, he sent an officer to check his story.

"He'll lie to you," Biff promised. "I never realized what trouble that guy was until we tried to hold up that convenience store. He was ready to put all the blame on Larry and me.

Would've gotten away with it, too, but the guys at juvie stood up for us. He had a worse record than anybody in the place."

"Glad you finally saw the error of your choice in friends," the chief said dryly. As the three started to leave, he commented, "Maybe I should hire Toot and Sweet. You're getting a reputation around town--like you always get your man."

"In this case, it was a canary," Sandy said.

"And a horse," Tim added.

As they walked out of the station, Biff said, "I can drop you off."

"Thanks," said Tim, who avoided walking whenever possible.

"Maybe you can meet Billy while you're in the neighborhood," Sandy suggested when he stopped the pickup in front of her house. "He'll want to thank you for helping get his canary back."

"He--ck. I was the guy took it in the first place."

"He doesn't need to know that."

Biff agreed, and they walked to Billy's house. Mona was sitting on the porch swing with her puppy when they passed. "Hi," she called. "Say hi, Pokey," she added. The puppy barked. Suddenly the little girls face looked curious. "Sandy," she began. Sandy looked from Mona to Biff, then back again.

"Looks sort of like him, I guess," she said to the little girl. "This is our friend Biff."

"Biff?" Mona giggled. "Like a biff on the nose?"

"No. Like, do nice things for people Biff. It's his nickname. Like this is Toot," she went on, pointing to Tim. "And I'm Sweet."

"Funny names," the little girl said. Pokey wriggled out of her arms and jumped down. "Come back ," she yelled, dashing after him.

"Thanks," said Biff. "Sounds like something I'll try to live up to."

When Billy ran out his door to greet them, Sandy said, "This is the man who helped get your canary back."

"Gee, thanks Mister," Billy said. He pointed toward Twinby's cage inside the closed window. "He's a happy birdie now."

"And you're a happy boy," Sandy said. Glancing toward her home, she saw her mother on the porch. "Why don't you all come in for lunch," she invited.

"Want to?" Sandy asked Tim and Biff. "You, too, Billy."

Biff looked uneasy, but Sandy urged him to join them. "Your new image will get off to a good start when you taste my mother's pizza."

They walked up the steps together, grinning at each other.

21

When Toot and Sweet next saw Biff, he was siting in the white pickup in front of Sandy's house. "They asked me down at the station if I'd like to go up and help recover the loot Butch's dad buried there. Don't know what I can do, but they said you guys were invited too."

Sandy yipped with delight. Tim grinned. "You driving up?" they both asked at the same time.

"That's the idea," he said, reaching across and opening the passenger's door. Tim waited for Sandy to climb up, then joined her. "Buckle up," Biff said. "There's two belts."

"Gosh, thanks," Tim said. Sandy almost bounced with excitement.

The young man revved the motor. He looked sort of embarrassed. "I don't see how I'm ever going to pay you back for getting me on the right track. My dad says you're finders of lost boys."

"We did find Billy Barnes when he went out to pet Thunder, but... ."

"Dad's thinking more along the line of you putting me back in school, if Peterson can swing it. You know, out of juvie and into the mainstream." He hesitated, then glanced at Sandy and asked, "Think you could--uh--sort of go with me when I talk to him?"

"Sure," she said. "We're having practice this afternoon. Why don't you come along? That's if we get back from Mission Bank Loot Rescue in time."

Biff nodded, gulping as if he found it impossible to speak. He swung the truck out onto the highway leading up the mountain. No one spoke for most of the drive. Finally, Tim asked, "What time are the police going to be there?"

His question was answered as Biff pulled to a stop in front of the general store. Toot and Sweet climbed out and walked toward Mr. Mason, who was on the front steps talking to Chief Shaw. "Never suspected a thing when those two were "interviewing" me. I guess that was their cover when they wanted to check out the mine. Kids can do remarkable things."

The police chief nodded agreement. "Speaking of super sleuths," he said, turning to Sandy and Tim, "have you sharpened your shovels?"

"You mean, we get to go down into the mine?" Sandy asked. Tim didn't seem to share her enthusiasm.

"Sorry. Too risky. We have someone out there now, but he's waiting for backup before he takes any chances. We'll have men on the spot to dig him out in case of another cave-in."

"We'd better get started," Sandy said. "It's not an easy

trail, takes almost an hour to get to the mine."

"Horses would be nice," Tim allowed, but he gamely fell in with Sandy as Chief Shaw motioned to Biff. They let Toot and Sweet take the lead.

Later Sandy breathed a sigh of relief when she saw the man emerge from the mine carrying two large bags. "How much is in them?" she wondered to Tim. He shrugged.

"Had to be a bundle for a guy like Butch to risk the mine falling in on him," he said, adding, "He told us a guy named Mullins was the one started spending some of the stolen money. We've got an APB out on him."

Tired from the hike, Sandy wondered about baseball practice. Would her arm be up to it? *Well*, she reasoned, *my legs did all the work. And they get to rest on the ride down the mountain.*

Before they got into the pickup again, Chief Shaw said to Tim and Sandy, "You two will get a reward for helping find this."

Sandy looked at Biff. "He's the one responsible for getting it back. The reward should be his."

Chief Shaw said, "Right. Part of it will go to Larson. We'll let you know the particulars when the bank in Cranden gets the money back." He was about to get into his car when he said, "By the way, Butch seems to have decided it would pay to coop- erate with the authorities. Gave us a description of the one named Larry. Right now, he's just happy to be getting out of the hospital in a day or two."

"And looking for me?" Biff asked.

"Probably not. I hope we've persuaded him to clean up his act. Told him not to try anything in Gainsburg if he doesn't want to end up in jail. He's old enough now to go to prison if he gets into any more trouble."

It was another silent drive down the mountain. Tim and

Sandy both fell asleep, wakening as Biff pulled to a stop at the ball park where practice was just starting.

"Oh," Sandy said, blinking. "We're here."

"Yep," Biff said.

"There's Coach," she noted.

"Yep," Biff said again.

He did not look confident as he and Sandy walked toward the dugout, where batters were doing practice swings. Coach Peterson turned to glance at Sandy.

"I'd just about given up on you. Got Jenner warming up," he said.

"I brought you another pitcher," she offered.

Biff looked almost ready to turn and run when Peterson held out a welcoming hand. "Could use a litte help coaching this afternoon," he said. "And then, we'll see what develops."

Tim slowly walked to the bleachers,where he settled down to watch. Walking home wasn't part of his plan.

22

It was a contented Biff who dropped Sandy and Tim off after practice. He had an appointment with Coach for the following day. He already knew he would be enrolling in summer school.

"Thanks," Tim said as he climbed out of the pickup.

"No, I am thanking you guys. I've got a life again."

Toot and Sweet watched him drive away. It was then they noticed a truck from the phone company parked in front of the Carpenter home. Shrugging, Sandy said, "Hope nothing's wrong with our phone. We don't want to miss any calls--business, that is."

"Speaking of business, I think we should write up the case of the missing canary," Tim said. "Let's go back to the office and do it now."

"Right," Sandy said, grinning. "Gotta keep the files up to date. Or should I say file? One case doesn't make a full cabinet."

"So you think we're 'One Case Wonders'?" Tim asked. "Will you be spreading the word we're out of business almost before we've begun?"

Joking, they stopped at the door to their office. It was *not* locked. It wasn't even closed. They dashed inside, then stopped abruptly. Kneeling near Tim's computer, a man was working with wires.

"What?" Tim asked. It was the only word he could manage. Sandy, too, was speechless.

The man glanced up and said, "You must be the famous detectives I've been hearing about."

His words brought Sandy out of her trance. "This is our office, yes. And what are you doing in it?"

"Seems some concerned citizen thought a business like yours needed its own phone. I'm installing it."

"We can't... ." began Tim.

"We're broke," Sandy said. "No way we can pay for this, much less the montly bill."

"Like I said, a concerned citizen is paying for installation. And another one has covered the bill for six months. That's unless you get into phoning China, or something."

Tim shook his head. "Do you mind telling us who these 'concerned citizens' are?"

The man pulled a paper out of his back pocket. "Guy named Larson. Owns the TV shop in town. He's doing the installation. A Mrs. Barnes is paying the bill for six months. Something about 'Billy owes you young people that much'."

"Mr. Larson?" Sandy gasped. "And Mrs. Barnes. We can't let them do this."

" 'S all paid for, kid. I'm just doing my job."

Tim sank down on one of the little chairs they'd kept until they could buy real office furniture. Sandy pulled up another and sat with her friend. "We have to talk to them," she said.

"Maybe the reward we'll get can cover it," Tim suggested.

Sandy relaxed a little. "Yeah, I guess."

When the man had gone, they sat and stared at each other for a while. Then Tim said, "I might as well type up the particulars of the case," but Sandy shook her head.

"I want to go to the TV shop and talk to Mr. Larson."

"Too late. Everything's closed," Tim said. "Besides, my stomach says it's dinner time."

Sandy agreed, but they decided it would be better for them to eat at their own homes. The hike in to the mine, and Sandy's practice had tired her out. As for Tim, the walk was more exercise than he had in any regular week. Nothing about life had been 'regular', though. Not since Toot and Sweet had gone into business. They agreed to meet after school the next day and bike to the TV shop.

"Or maybe we should just call Mr. Larson from our new phone," Sandy said. "It seems only fair the first call should be to the man who made it possible."

"I can stop and talk to Mrs. Barnes on my way home," Tim said.

However, when they met in the office the next day the phone rang before they could make a call. Both reached to answer it, but Tim played the gentleman and gave Sandy the honors.

"Chief Shaw," she said. "How did you know our new number? Or even know we had a phone?" She held the receiver so Tim could hear, too.

"My spies are everywhere," he said with a chuckle.

"Actually, I had to see Larson about getting a new TV, and he told me what he was doing to express his appreciation for all you did for Biff."

"We didn't really do anything," Sandy protested

"Larson seems to think otherwise. But that's not why I called. The bank in Cranden wants to deposit a thousand dollars to your account. They're transferring the money to our bank. And it's open for about another hour. Can you make it down there to set up an account, fill in signatures, all the busy work?"

"Can we?" Tim shouted. "We're on our bikes."

They rode so fast they would have broken speed limits if there were any for bicycles. But for Sandy's caution, Tim would have run the red light on Maynard Street. Parking their bikes in the rack in front of First National Bank, they dashed inside. A 'New Accounts' officer motioned them to her desk.

"Yes," they said. "The account is under the name Toot Sweet Detective Agency."

"Yes," they said. "Both our signatures."

When the business was finished, the woman smiled. "Cranden State Bank will deposit one thousand dollars to this account at the beginning of the business day tomorrow."

On the way out the door Tim said, "I'd pinch you if I didn't think you'd yip. You do that, you know."

"And why do I deserve a pinch?" Sandy demanded.

"We both do. How else will we know we aren't dreaming?"

"Let's go by the TV shop," Sandy said. "I want to know if Biff got a reward too."

"Chief Shaw said he would," Tim reminded her. "Besides, we can call from our office."

"Okay," Sandy agreed. "We're pretty official now, with a

phone *and* a bank account. I guess we'll have to print up new business cards, since we can take calls in our office."

"We can even pay for an answering machine to take messages when we have to be at school," Tim said.

They rode home, no longer feeling the need to speed. When they went into the office, Sandy said, "Now we'll make our first phone call. The one from Chief Shaw was an *incoming call*. This will be our first *outgoing call*. And I want it to be to Mr. Larson."

As she spoke, the phone rang. This time, it was Tim's turn to answer.

"Toot Sweet Detective Agency," he said. His face registered shock as he listened to the voice on the other end of the line.

"What is it?" Sandy demanded.

His hand trembled when he put down the phone. "We have our next case," he said. "Someone is on his way over to talk to us about--," Tim frowned-- "a thirteenth floor?"

"Where? A hotel? Nobody ever has a thirteenth floor," Sandy said.

"You know as much about this case as I do. He did say he'd pay us an advance. And that our investigation would take us out of town."

"That could present a problem with our parents." Sandy saw difficulties only as something to be overcome. "Things worked out when we needed to go to the mine, so we'll get around it somehow."

"Pretty professional, getting an advance," Tim said.

Sandy agreed. "Yippee," she shouted. "Toot and Sweet are in business again."

Tim grabbed her hands, and together they dance around the office. Whatever they might have planned had been forgotten.

Then practical Sandy said, "When are they coming? Today? We'd better get serious, tout de suite. I've learned the French, you know."

"Right," Tim agreed. "ASAP"